EXPRESS NEWSPAPERS plc, Ludgate House,
245 Blackfriars Road,
London SE1 9UX

Produced by Brainwaves Limited
5 Highwood Ridge, Hatch Warren, Basingstoke,
Hampshire RG22 4UU.

ISBN 0–85079–244–4

RUPERT

and the Pirate Treasure

One day Rupert receives a note from his old friend
Sailor Sam. "Come quickly," says the note, "There
is something I want you to see." Rupert runs all
the way to Sam's wooden cabin, on the edge of
Nutwood Village.

Sam is waiting for him at the garden gate. "What is
it?" asks Rupert. "It's a sailing boat, I found it
in an old sea-chest," says Sam, showing Rupert the
old boat. "Just look at this," says Rupert, as he
lifts the sail. "Whatever could it be?"

The treasure is on an island not far from Rocky Bay. "Let's go and look for it," says Rupert excitedly. So, they drive down to Rocky Bay in Sam's old car. They are so busy getting Sam's boat ready to sail, that they don't notice two pirates hiding behind a barrel on the quayside.

Unknown to Sam and Rupert, the pirates hear the chums talking about the treasure. As soon as Sam's boat is ready to sail, Rupert and Sam head out towards the open sea to start their treasure hunt.

It's a beautiful day for sailing, and Sam's little boat speeds through the water. The sky is blue and there's a stiff breeze. Soon, they are joined by a school of playful dolphins. "Hello!" calls Rupert as he watches them leap out of the water.

Suddenly it begins to grow dark. Ahead of them lies a big cloud of thick fog. "Oh dear!" says Sam. "It's so foggy I can't tell where we are." "Don't worry," says Rupert. "The dolphins seem to be showing us the way."

They sail out into the bright sunshine and head towards the island. Sam anchors his boat and the two jump out. Rupert takes charge of the treasure map while Sam carries a shovel.

"It can't be very far from here," says Rupert, looking at the map. Soon they find the place where the treasure should be and Sam begins to dig. Down and down he digs until there's a loud clunk as his shovel hits something hard. There, at the bottom of the hole, is a big slab of stone.

Sam hauls out the heavy chest to let Rupert see the
treasure. The chest is full of gold and silver
coins, rubies, diamonds and pearls. "Goodness!"
exclaims Rupert, "It must have been buried here by
pirates." "It may have been, long ago. But there
can't be any pirates around here now," replies Sam.

No sooner has Sam spoken than they both hear a
rustling sound in the trees nearby. "Hush!" says
Sam. "I think we're being watched." "But who else
could be here on the island?" asks Rupert.

"We'll take charge of that!" laugh the pirates and make Sam and Rupert drag the treasure chest down to the beach. As they lift the lid and start to count the treasure, Rupert sees his chance to escape and runs off as fast as he can.

He races along the beach until he spots a large seashell, lying in the sand. Rupert raises the shell to his lips like a trumpet and blows with all his might! Sam hears the sound and wonders who Rupert could be calling . . .

Before the wicked pirates can run away, they are
seized by the sea serpents and lifted high into
the air. Rupert races back to Sam, who is showing
the Merboy the chest of treasure.

The Merboy tells Rupert and Sam that all pirate
treasure rightly belongs to his master, King
Neptune. As they are talking, the sea suddenly
begins to froth and boil and a huge wave appears in
the bay nearby. "Don't worry," says the Merboy.
"You have nothing to fear."

King Neptune lands on the shore and orders the sea
serpents to take the two pirates to a faraway
island, where they can cause no more trouble.

Rupert and Sam load the treasure chest into King
Neptune's chariot. He thanks them both and waves
goodbye, as he sets off across the sea to his
underwater kingdom. "Come on Rupert," says Sam,
"It's a long sail home to Rocky Bay." "Don't
worry," says the Merboy, "I'll soon have you home
in no time!"